First published in Belgium and Holland by Clavis Uitgeverij, Hasselt – Amsterdam, 2015
Copyright © 2015, Clavis Uitgeverij

English translation from the Dutch by Clavis Publishing Inc. New York
Copyright © 2016 for the English language edition: Clavis Publishing Inc. New York

Visit us on the web at www.clavisbooks.com

Princess Lemonella written by Saarein te Brake and illustrated by Sassafras De Bruyn
Original title: *Prinses Piccalilly*
Translated from the Dutch by Clavis Publishing

ISBN 978-1-60537-291-4

This book was printed in August 2016 at Publikum d.o.o., Slavka Rodica 6, Belgrade, Serbia

First Edition
10 9 8 7 6 5 4 3 2 1

Saarein te Brake & Sassafras De Bruyn

Princess Lemonella

Clavis

NEW YORK

One day a little princess was born in the kingdom of Cornichon. The king and queen were over the moon about their daughter! They called her Ella.

"Coochie coochie coo,"
the king laughed.
"Have you ever seen such a pretty princess?"
the queen exclaimed.

But what was that?
The king and queen exchanged a surprised look
and leaned over the crib again.

Was that a frown between her eyes?
Why did the princess press
her lips together so?
Her arms were crossed
and she definitely looked grumpy!

The king lifted the princess out of her crib
and playfully threw her in the air.
But Princess Ella had a sour look.
The queen made silly faces.
But Princess Ella still had a sour look.
They brought in a clown, a musician,
a bear on a bicycle.
But Princess Ella still had a sour look.

"We have such a grouchy daughter,"
the king and queen sighed.
"From now on," they said,
"we'll call her Princess Lemonella."

Princess Lemonella grew up.
She went to school.
She went to parties.
But she didn't smile.
She kept her lips firmly pressed together,
crossed her arms
and sat sour-faced in her tower room.

After eighteen sour years the king and queen decided
it was time for Princess Lemonella to get married.
They hoped for a dapper, lighthearted prince.
Maybe he could make their daughter laugh.
"Wanted - Happy prince!" said posters everywhere.

One day a prince on a beautiful
white horse approached.
"Hello," he said with a smile, "I'm Prince Hans."
He rode toward the princess's tower room.
"Princess Lemonella!" he sang.
"Throw your golden braid out of the window!
I'll climb up and we'll live happily ever after!"

Princess Lemonella looked in the mirror.
"Do I have to?" she sighed.
"I don't like it when someone pulls my hair.
And I don't even have a braid."
The princess ignored the first prince and did nothing.

Shortly afterwards, a prince
in a shiny golden coach approached.
He got out and walked toward the princess's tower room.
He had a pink slipper in his hands.
"Princess Lemonella!" he called brightly.
"I found a pink slipper on the steps of my palace.
Come downstairs, so we can find out if it fits you.
We'll have a wonderful future together!"

Princess Lemonella looked at her feet.
"Do I have to?" she sighed.
"I've just put on these lovely warm socks."
The princess ignored the second prince and did nothing.

After a while another prince arrived.
He dragged a huge bed behind him.
It had at least twenty mattresses piled on top of each other!
The prince walked toward the princess's tower room.
"Princess Lemonella," he said solemnly.
"Sleep on this pile of mattresses for me tonight.
Tomorrow, at the crack of dawn, you'll become my wife!"

Princess Lemonella rolled over in her warm bed.
I'm comfortable here, she thought.
Why would I move to another bed?
The princess ignored the third prince and did nothing.

The king and queen
didn't touch their dinner that evening.
"It's not working," the king sighed.
"She doesn't want a prince," the queen whined.
Princess Lemonella sat in a corner.
With a sour look on her face.

The next morning Princess Lemonella
was leaning out of the window
when she saw a little dot in the distance.
The little dot became a young man on a horse.
The young man came closer.
And closer.
And rode past her!

"Hey!" Princess Lemonella yelled.
"Hey, you! Don't you want to ask
if I can hang my golden braid out of the window?
Or if I want to try on a slipper?
Or if I want to sleep on twenty mattresses?
Hey! Hello!"

The young man rode toward Princess Lemonella.
"Do I have to?" he sighed.
"Where am I supposed to find a slipper? Or a mattress?
You can hang your braid out of the window if you want to,
but I'm moving on."

Princess Lemonella looked him up and down.
Was that a frown between his eyes?
Why did he press his lips together like that?
Were his arms actually crossed?

"Where are you going?" Princess Lemonella asked.
"To find a princess," the young man answered.
"A cheerful one:
that's what my mom and dad want for me.
But I can't find a cheerful princess anywhere."

"Oh," Princess Lemonella said. "How unpleasant. Well, good luck to you, Prince eh...? What's your name?"

"I'm Prince Peter," the prince answered, "but my mom and dad call me Prince Pickle."

"I'm Princess Lemonella," the princess said. And they shook hands.

"Funny name you got there," the prince noticed.

"Well, yours is too," the princess answered.

And then they started laughing.

At first, they laughed carefully,
because the corners of the princess's mouth
were always sliding back down
and the arms of the prince kept crossing.
But after a while they laughed heartily. They couldn't stop!
Together, they walked toward the princess's tower room.

And you can still hear their laughter all over the kingdom....